My Llama Steals the Show Every Time

Written and Illustrated by
Tani Adams

This book belongs to:

_____

This book is dedicated to my amazing, talented and fun-loving daughters, Paige and Mackenzie. Thank you for dragging me to your dance classes, dance recitals and llama shows. Thank you for your kindness, patience, love and hard work raising our llamas and alpacas. I have enjoyed watching you girls grow up. I will cherish every minute of every day. I would not change a thing.

Love,

Mom

My Llama Steals the Show Every Time

Copyright © 2021 Tani Adams.

iUniverse
1663 Liberty Drive
Bloomington, IN 47403
www.iuniverse.com
844-349-9409

ISBN: 978-1-6632-1764-6 (sc)
978-1-6632-1796-7 (hc)
978-1-6632-1765-3 (e)

Library of Congress Control Number: 2021901580

iUniverse rev. date: 03/12/2021

My Llama Steals the Show Every Time

Written and Illustrated by
Tani Adams

Dancing and dancing
to the talent SHOW we go...
I can't wait to be in the SHOW!

OH no! OH no!
Where did that silly,
Llama-Llama,
of mine go?

It is **only** one hour
before the **show!**

We must be going!
There is no time to play…
No Llama-Llama…
Not in the hay!

OH,
Llama-Llama!
Time to load
up the trailer!
Time to Race
off to the
SHOW.
Let's REV up
the engine!
LET'S GET ON
THE ROAD...

Nana's
Leap'n Llamas
Ranch

Llama-Llama
Please take your place.
Please stay in line.
The Man in the BIG HAT,
will let YOU know
when it is your time...

OH no,
OH no!
It is not her turn
Not her time to
go...
My silly
Llama-Llama
Always Steals the
show.

"Don't Feed the Bears,
Don't feed the bears,
I say!
Bears will Raid your camp by night
and Raid your CAR by day...
Please put all your food up high
to keep the bears away..."

"Hey Llama-Llama

COME back with my BASKET!"

No matter WHERE WE GO...

NO MATTER WHO WE KNOW

WHEN MY LLAMA COMES TO TOWN

PEOPLE GATHER AROUND

MY
SILLY
HAPPY
DANCING
SINGING
LITTLE
Llama-
Llama

ALWAYS...

STEALS the SHOW
Every Time!

The End

How to draw a llama

Step One:
Using a pencil and a piece of tracing paper. Lay the paper on top of this page; connect the dots. Using the graph can help with getting the eyes ears and mouth Lined up.

Step Two: Add llama Hair to head, neck and body

Step Three:
Draw the eyes and the eyelashes and a tutu.

Step Four:
Color your llama

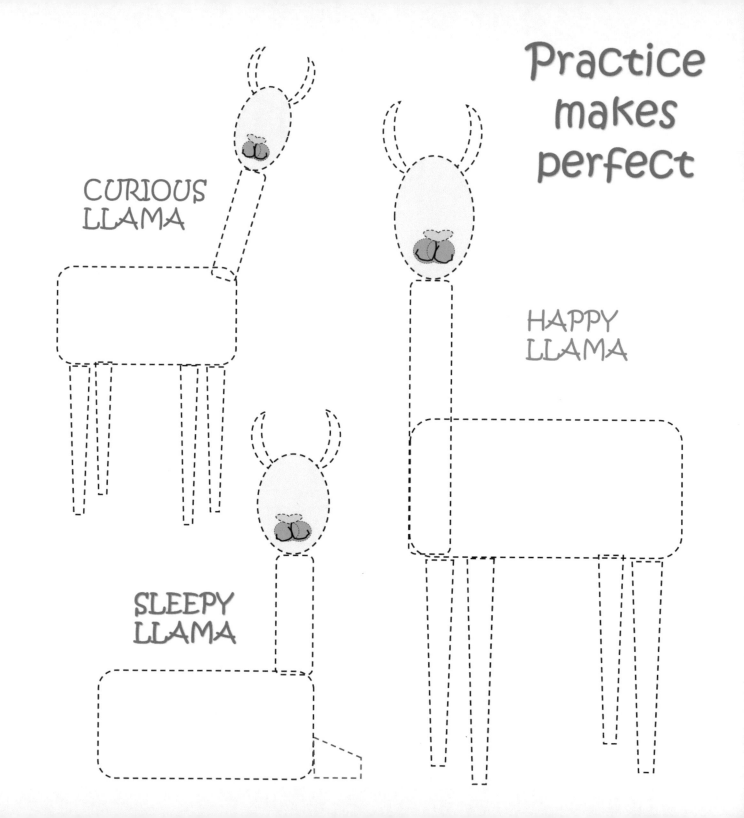

CURIOUS
LLAMA

Practice
makes
perfect

HAPPY
LLAMA

SLEEPY
LLAMA

Llama Writing

Llama

dance

tutu

sing

act

Practice makes perfect

act dance sing tutu

About the Author

I live in the Pacific Northwest and have had the privilege to own and raise llamas. I had an opportunity to go hiking with some friends who had llamas that were used for packing all our gear for the day. These animals were majestic, sweet and carefree creatures with a soothing Humm which was how I grew to love llamas. I am the illustrator of this book and I taught myself how to draw. I also have a background in graphic design. I had a dream to one day become an author for children's books and to get published. I have many more books planned to be released and hope to visit your local library for a book signing and a reading.

I have llamas of my own and have been known for walking my llamas into town for coffee and carrots. Coffee for me and carrots for my llamas. People would stop whatever they were doing to come see us during our walks. They would ask questions about llamas and alpacas like "Where do Llamas come from? Do llamas spit? Can you ride a llama? The most asked question was "Can I pet the llama? The public loved taking pictures with the llama, feeding the llamas, or being surprised when they were kissed by a llama! I have made many costumes for my llamas and my llamas periodically have been seen wearing a Tutu... Enjoy the book!

Tani Adams

Author's
Autograph

My Llama Steals the Show Every Time

This book is a story of a little llama who loves to dance and sing. She lives on "Leaping Llama Ranch". She lives with Nana, Lola and some other little critters. Llama-Llama Tutu's best friend is a little red rooster who likes to follow her wherever she goes. Nana calls her "Llama-Llama", but her full name is "Llama-Llama Tutu". There is a talent show and Nana has entered Llama-Llama Tutu in a talent show. It is not an easy task keeping a llama clean and getting the llama into the trailer, so they can get to the talent show in time. Llama-llama Tutu is in the Finale, Llama-llama Tutu is supposed to wait her turn, but just can't sit still and ends up in all the acts.

Trademark
Of llama-llama 2.2

This is the real Llama-llama Tutu, who is also known as Invec. Invee is very smart and loves going to shows. As a team we would perform at Llama shows with other llama friends from around the United States. Invee could never stand still in the show ring and was always dancing around when the judges were looking. I believe if it wasn't for her soft fluffy fleece and her conformation. She might not have received an award. It is true that if you devote time handling and building a positive relationship with your llama, in return they love and respect you. Showing a llama love, patience, respect and understanding; llamas can be sweet, gentle creatures.

Printed in the United States
by Baker & Taylor Publisher Services